Praise for Storyshares

"One of the brightest innovators and game-changers in the education industry."
— Forbes

"Your success in applying research-validated practices to promote literacy serves as a valuable model for other organizations seeking to create evidence-based literacy programs."   — Library of Congress

"We need powerful social and educational innovation, and Storyshares is breaking new ground. The organization addresses critical problems facing our students and teachers. I am excited about the strategies it brings to the collective work of making sure every student has an equal chance in life."
— Teach For America

"It's the perfect idea. There's really nothing like this. I mean, wow, this will be a wonderful experience for young people."   — Andrea Davis Pinkney,
Executive Director, Scholastic

"Reading for meaning opens opportunities for a lifetime of learning. Providing emerging readers with engaging texts that are designed to offer both challenges and support for each individual will improve their lives for years to come. Storyshares is a wonderful start."
— David Rose, Co-founder of CAST & UDL

The Trading Card Queen

Published by Storyshares, LLC
Inspiring reading with a new kind of book.

Storyshares
Storyshares, LLC
24 N. Bryn Mawr Avenue #340
Bryn Mawr, Pennsylvania 19010-3304
www.storyshares.org

Interest Level: High School
Grade Level Equivalent: 1.7

ISBN 9798885977128
Book design by Saskia Globig

Storyshares presents

The Trading Card Queen

Sandra Morris

Storyshares

Chapter One

Nina felt like she could fly home.

Not fly like the dragons on her trading cards.

Float.

Nina felt like the dragonfly that landed on a flower near the high school.

Its black body and bright blue wings were pretty against the stone path.

A dragonfly didn't worry about much. It just thought about where it would land next. People didn't scream and run away when they saw a dragonfly. They didn't swat it away.

It must have been a happy life.

And today, Nina felt like she was a dragonfly.

This morning, she had a stack of trading cards in her backpack.

Now the stack was gone.

She only had one trading card left. It was a special one.

This didn't worry her. She would make more.

She was the trading card queen.

And this is her story.

Chapter Two

Every day after class, Nina walked to the grade school to pick up Ben. She loved her little brother. She didn't love this chore.

Other kids in tenth grade played on a tennis or soccer team. Maybe Nina could next year. That's what her mother promised.

Things would get better now. They were safe and had a new home in the United States. Her mom took a second job to help pay Ben's hospital bills. While her mother was at work, Nina had to watch Ben after school.

Nina knew better in her heart. Next year, something else would go wrong. Ben might go to the hospital again. If he did, mom would be with him. Then she might lose her job. They would have to move if they didn't pay the rent.

Something always went wrong. Besides, Nina would never make a team. She didn't know how to throw, kick, or cheer.

Sometimes she wished she did! She wished she had friends to walk with in the halls. She wanted to be someone else. Not the new girl from far away. The girl who got her school clothes from Goodwill.

No one was mean to her. She didn't give them the chance.

She looked away when they looked at her. She walked with her head down in the hall. At lunch, she stayed in the bathroom. If someone came in, she pretended to brush her hair. She didn't need to eat lunch alone if she stayed there.

Back in her old hometown, her friends had fun after school. Some worked, and some played a sport. They thought Nina was lucky to move to the United States. She could have a good life. They dreamed of being with Nina. Nina dreamed of being back with them.

Nina moved to the United States at the start of the school year. It had been five weeks. Nina hadn't met a single friend.

Nina missed her old home. There, she had friends. Now, she felt all alone. She decided not to make friends. She was scared of being turned away.

Chapter Three

Ben came out of the school before the rest of his class. This rule was for kids with special needs. They said it would stop him from getting hurt in a big group. Nina thought it was so Ben could feel what it was like to be first.

He ran to her. She could see something was wrong. His body was too tiny for his age. If he could just have the operation he needed. Then his cancer would be gone.

Today, his face was sad. He had red cheeks and a runny nose. He was crying.

"They took my dragon card!" he said.

His tears fell on her faded t-shirt. She wiped
his dripping nose. She wiped the soggy cracker
crumbs from his shirt.

"Who did?" she asked.

"I did," a voice said.

She stood to see Ben's teacher, Mr. Burns. He
held the trading card. Nina grabbed it from him.
He raised his eyebrows at her anger. She didn't
mean to be rude. She didn't want it to be gone for
good.

"I'm sorry. It's all my fault," she said. "I didn't
know it was against the rules. Please don't tell
our mother."

"Where did he get the card?" Mr. Burns asked.

Nina looked down at the dragon with its wide,
bright green wings.

"I made it for him," she said.

"He should leave it at home. Everyone in class
wanted to have it. It might get lost here."

Or stolen. He didn't say that out loud. Still, Nina knew it was the truth.

"I promise it won't happen again," she said.

She put the card into her brother's jacket pocket. He looked up at her like she was a rock star.

Nina had a warm feeling in her belly.

Everyone in class wanted to have it.

Nina felt special. Even if no one knew her name.

Chapter Four

Nina made her first trading card when she was thirteen. They still lived in their old country.

At first, they were simple cards. She used crayon nubs and cardboard from the garbage. She would copy real cards with baseball and soccer stars.

Trading cards were a big deal at her school. Everyone kept a pocket full of special cards if they had some. No one ever traded unless they had two alike. That almost never happened.

Nina's art got better. Her teacher let her use markers from the special, locked closet. There were markers of all sizes and colors. There were stacks of shiny, thick paper.

If Nina had the money, she would have an art closet. It would feel like a treasure every time she looked inside. She would take special care of her pens and pencils. She would never break one. She would never leave a cap off her markers.

At the end of the year, the teacher let Nina take home stuff that was too worn to keep. The markers were dry and didn't work well. The less popular colors were almost like new. Paper with scribbles on one side was okay with Nina. She didn't care if someone drew hearts and flowers on the other side.

The markers were better than magic. Nina could make anything she wanted. Walking home with that box was one of the best days of her life.

It didn't last. The next week, Ben got sick for the first time.

Chapter Five

At first, Nina was angry at Ben. When he got sick, everything changed.

No one cared what Nina wanted. Their mother spent all her time at the hospital with Ben. When she came home, she went right to bed. She asked Nina to do the dishes and sweep the floor. Nina spent hours alone. No one seemed to care if she was happy.

She wasn't happy at all, but she didn't cry. Mother looked sad and tired. She was giving all her time and love to Ben. Nina felt like she didn't exist. She grew angry with Ben for getting sick. His cancer messed things up when life was getting good.

After a few weeks, Nina could see Ben at the hospital. Then she stopped being angry at him. She became angry at the world.

He had lost all his hair. His face was pale. There were dark circles under his eyes. He begged her to hug him to sleep, just like she did at home. The nurse smiled and said it was ok, so Nina did. She lay next to him and read him a story. Soon, there wasn't a book left to read.

The next day, she brought her art box with her to the hospital. While Ben watched, she would draw a card. There were dragons, and castles, and boys who rode great big horses. There was even a big sister with a magic cape.

She learned to go slow and work on the fine lines. She picked colors with care. The cards looked like the real cards she saw on the school playground. The kind people bought in a store.

Her art got better and better. After a while, Ben got better too. He was finally ready to leave the hospital.

The doctors said Ben needed a special operation. If he could have the operation, he would be okay. Nina watched her mom sit in the kitchen all that night. Then she heard her mother make a phone call. She talked a long time with Grandmother. Grandma lived in the United States.

In the morning, Nina went into the kitchen. She wanted a bowl of cereal.

"Nina, we need to speak," her mother said.

Nina knew what her mother was going to say. They were moving to the United States.

Nina said goodbye to her friends. She packed her bags. It was a very sad time in her life.

Chapter Six

Nina started the school year in a new country. Here in her new school, it was Friday. She hid in the bathroom during lunch break. She was happy for the weekend. Her mother said they could go to Goodwill to find more markers.

"Nina?" she heard someone call in the hall.

She didn't turn around. No one knew her there. They must have been calling to someone else.

"Nina? Hello!"

This time, Nina stopped. Maybe it was her teacher. Did she leave something behind on her desk?

The girl who called her name stopped in front of her and smiled.

"There you are! Did you hear me calling you?" the girl asked.

Nina didn't know what to say. Who was this girl? What did she want? Nina hadn't done anything wrong.

"I'm Jenny Burns. My father teaches your brother, Ben."

Nina still didn't speak. Was Ben in trouble? Then she grew worried. Did Ben get sick at school?

"What's wrong?" Nina asked.

"Nothing is wrong. My dad said he saw some of your art. He said you were really good. I wanted to invite you to the Art Club."

Jenny pushed a card into Nina's hands.

The bell rang, and lunch was over.

Nina put the card in her backpack. She had never been part of a club before. An art club would be so fun!

She knew her mother would say no. They didn't have the money. And who would watch Ben?

Nina thought about the club all the way home. She pulled the card out of her backpack and read it. The club met on Saturday mornings. That was when Nina watched Ben so their mother could go buy food.

It would never work out. But it had been nice to have someone call her by name. Maybe Nina would say hello to Jenny if she saw her in the hall.

She put the card on the kitchen table next to her artwork. Ben was asking for a peanut butter cracker snack. Nina forgot about the note and took care of her brother.

Chapter Seven

"Nina, what is this?" asked her mother.

Nina opened her eyes. It was Saturday morning and Ben was still asleep.

Mother stood in the bedroom door with the art club card in her hand.

"Nothing, Mom. I know I can't go," Nina said.

"Nina. Get dressed. Ben can go with me today. This club will be good for you."

Nina sat up. Did her mother really say she could join a club?

"It might cost money," Nina said.

She hung her head in shame. It was hard to ask her mother for money when they had so many bills.

"I will find a way," her mother said. "Get dressed, Nina. It's time for you to find some friends."

Chapter Eight

Nina didn't know so many kids hung out at school on a Saturday.

There were kids playing soccer outside and kids playing basketball inside. Someone was playing a drum in the band room.

Nina stopped at the art room door. She didn't know what she would find. Maybe no one would be there. Maybe there was no art club. Could this have been a mean joke?

Jenny was there with a group of other students about Nina's age.

"There you are!" said Jenny. "Everyone, this is Nina!"

Soon, Nina knew the names of everyone in the club. They all made her feel like she was part of the group. They called her by her name.

"We need to make some money for the club," Jenny said. "Let's come up with some ideas. Then we can vote on the best one."

Nina felt better. It didn't sound like she would need to ask her mother for money. But what could they do to make money for art supplies?

Everyone came up with an idea. They had all known each other for a long time. They all got along and worked together. Only Nina was new. She was afraid to speak in case they laughed at her.

She looked out the window at the soccer team. The band played down the hall.

"We could offer face painting at the games again," a boy named Josh said.

"We did that last year," Jenny said. "It's good. I wish we could do something new. Nina, do you have an idea?"

Nina watched the soccer team. She listened to the band. Then she took a deep breath.

"We could make trading cards," she said.

No one said a word.

"What kind of trading cards?" Josh asked. "Who would buy them?"

"They would." Nina pointed to the soccer team. "If the dragons on the cards were wearing soccer shirts."

Jenny smiled.

Josh patted Nina on the back.

"And bears with pom-poms!" someone else piped up.

"And a card for the swim team!" Jenny stood up. "Great work, Nina! I think we just found a winner!"

Chapter Nine

The club still had work to do. There were twelve people in the club. Each person needed to make a card. It had to be their best art.

There would be twelve different cards. The art would go to the school print shop. The print shop would put all twelve works of art on one page. Then they would print everything on big pieces of glossy, thick paper. There would be one hundred sets of cards.

Once the print was dry, each page needed to be cut into the trading cards.

"That's a lot of cards," said Jenny.

"How much will a pack of cards cost?" asked Josh.

"We should make sure we cover the price of paper," said Jenny.

"And the cost of printing the cards," said Nina.

"The print shop said it would cost fifty dollars for the whole job," said Josh.

"Let's sell them for twenty dollars a pack!" someone said. "We could be rich!"

Most people in the club seemed to like that idea.

"I think we should sell them for less. Then everyone who wants to can have a set," said Nina. She wasn't happy about making people feel left out. She knew all about wanting something you couldn't buy.

Josh was doing math on a piece of scrap paper.

"If we sell a hundred packs for five dollars each, we will make five hundred dollars," he said.

"Then we pay the print shop fifty dollars. That leaves us with four hundred fifty dollars," said Jenny.

"That would be our best year ever!" said Josh.
"Can we do this? Really?"

Everyone looked at Nina. She felt nervous. What if
this didn't work out? Would they blame her?

"I think we should try," she said.

The club took a vote.

Everyone wanted to give the idea a try. They
asked Nina to decide what trading cards they
should make.

She said she would bring the list in the next day.

Chapter Ten

After helping Ben with his homework, Nina set the table for dinner. She had her homework done, but she needed to come up with a list of trading card names.

It was scary to have everyone counting on her. It seemed fun to be part of an art club. Being the leader made her feel afraid. Would they blame her if it didn't go well? What if they didn't like the trading card she asked them to draw? It seemed like more to worry about. Nina already had enough worry.

Ben wanted to help. He kept asking her what she was doing. After dinner, she sat at the table with her notes out. When Ben leaned in to watch, his glass of milk spilled all over her notes.

"Ben!" Nina cried. "Look what you have done! I wish you would stop bugging me!"

"Nina! He was just trying to help!" their mother said.

Ben looked at Nina with sad eyes. Nina felt like crying, too. It wasn't fair. No matter what, Ben always came first. If he wasn't happy, everyone wanted to help make it better. If Nina wasn't happy, it didn't matter to anyone.

Nina went to her room. Maybe she would just stop being in the club. It would be easier that way.

Chapter Eleven

"You can't just quit," Josh said after school the next day.

"Yes, I can. This isn't going to work," said Nina as she walked to pick up Ben.

"I can help you come up with the list. Let's do it now." Josh kept following her.

"I can't. I need to pick up my brother." Nina wished Josh would go away.

She didn't want him to see Ben. She didn't want him to see her home. It was all too much. Would he ask why her brother was so small and pale? What if he laughed at their home?

"I'll go with you," Josh said.

"I wish you would just leave me alone," said Nina.

This was the worst. She didn't want to be mean,
but she was tired of acting like everything was ok.

They were in front of Ben's school. It was too late.
Ben was running to her with open arms.

"Nina. My Nina. Are you still mad at me?"
Ben asked.

Nina knew he was still thinking about the night
before. Her love was all that mattered to him. He
didn't care if she was a cheerleader. He didn't care
if she had a lot of friends.

Ben loved her just the way she was. Nina knew
she would never be angry with Ben again. He was
just too special.

"How could I be mad at you, Ben?" She picked him
up in a hug.

"Hey, little man!" Josh said behind her.

Nina forgot he was still there!

"Are you My Nina's friend?" asked Ben.

Josh looked at Nina and smiled. "I am. She doesn't know it, but I am."

Ben invited Josh to come home with them for saltines and peanut butter. Nina was sure he would say no. But Josh took Ben by the hand.

Soon, Nina was listening to Ben and Josh at the kitchen table while she poured milk. Ben was telling Josh about their whole life. Josh acted like he was glad to be there. Ben showed Josh all the trading cards Nina had made over the years.

"This is my favorite," said Ben, holding up the dragon.

"I can see why!" said Josh.

"My Nina!" said Ben. "She is the trading card queen!"

Josh and Nina both laughed. Nina hoped maybe things would really be okay this time.

Chapter Twelve

An hour later, Josh left for home.

They had worked together on a list of names:

Jenny: Swim team seals

Nina: Soccer team dragons

Max: Band club bears

Tasha: Basketball giraffes

Larry: Track club unicorns

Bruce: Tennis club tigers

Patty: Cheerleading pixies

Grace: French club lions

Debbie: Football team wizards

Randy: Print club rattlesnakes

Candy: Computer club owls

Josh: Art club...

Josh said he had an idea for their art club card, but it was a secret. He whispered the secret to Ben, and Ben just smiled. After Josh left, Nina hugged Ben. She thanked him for being such a good little brother.

Ben left soggy saltines on her t-shirt, and she didn't bother to brush them away this time.

Chapter Thirteen

Nina worked on her card all week. Ben helped by sitting next to her and handing her a pen when she asked. She told him he was a very good helper.

The cards needed to be done by the end of the week. Nina was close to being done. She was happy with what she had made. Ben said it was her very best card ever.

On Thursday, when they came home from school, Nina's mother was waiting for them. She should have been at work. Something must be wrong. Nina knew Ben wasn't sick because he was right next to her.

"Mom?" Nina called out when they went inside.

They found their mother in Ben's room. She was packing a bag.

"Mom?" asked Nina again.

She held Ben next to her. Something was happening, and it made Nina worry.

But when their mother turned to face them, she was smiling.

"The hospital called. Ben can have his operation."

Chapter Fourteen

Hugging Ben goodbye was the hardest thing Nina ever had to do. Her brother was a pain, but that didn't matter. Nina told him she loved him. She said she would see him soon.

"Can we make a new set of trading cards?" he asked. He touched her hair with his sticky hands.

"As many as you want," said Nina.

Grandmother was at the door. She would stay with Nina while Ben was in the hospital. Mother would stay with Ben.

Before Nina knew it, they were gone.

She sat on her bed and held Ben's dragon card. He left it behind to keep it safe.

She knew she should finish her art club card. She had too much going on inside her heart. The card was the last thing on her worry list.

Chapter Fifteen

Nina spent her Friday lunch hour in the bathroom.
She hadn't skipped lunch in a long time. The
art club always sat together. It was nice to have
friends who saved a seat for you.

Today, she wanted to be alone. She was thinking
about Ben. Was he ok? Was he feeling sick, or
scared?

Oh, how she wished she could be with him.

"Nina, are you in here?"

Jenny came into the bathroom.

Nina wiped away her tears and hid her face.

Jenny didn't leave. She asked what was wrong. Nina didn't share at first. She was afraid Jenny wouldn't care.

But Jenny wasn't that kind of friend. She stayed with Nina and held her hand as Nina talked about Ben. After school she even walked with Nina home. It was hard to walk right home and not stop to pick up Ben.

Nina would never be angry about taking care of Ben after school again.

Chapter Sixteen

Grandmother let her work on her art late that night. Nina finished her trading card.

Then she started a card for Ben. She wanted a new card to give to him when he came home.

The phone rang early on Saturday morning. It was her mother.

Grandmother talked to her for a few minutes, then handed the phone to Nina.

Ben had made it through the operation. He was going to be okay.

Chapter Seventeen

Nina was tired, but she went to the art club room the next day.

Ben was going to be okay. That was all that mattered. The cards were fun, and she hoped they would all sell. But it was just money. Having Ben feel good was better than money.

There was a plate of cookies on the art room table. There was also a get-well card for Ben. It was nice to have friends who cared about her little brother.

All twelve cards were done. They put their art on a big board to go to the print shop. Josh put his art on last. It was the trading card named for the

art club. He had painted a picture of Nina with
a cape and a crown.

"Our Nina," he said. "Our Trading Card Queen."

Chapter Eighteen

On a Saturday two weeks later, the art club held the big sale. They had cut the cards and put them in packs. Each club member needed to sell at least eight packs. That would be ninety-six packs of cards.

That would leave four packs of cards out of the one hundred they had printed. The four members of the print shop club really liked the cards.

Jenny made a deal with them. She gave them each a set of cards in trade for the printing. That saved the art club fifty dollars.

It was a really good trade.

Nina stood at the side of the soccer field. Josh stood at the snack stand. Jenny stood outside the school gym. They all had a place.

Would this really work?

At first Nina was afraid. Then she thought of Ben. These cards were just for fun.

"Trading cards!" she called out. "Trading cards for five dollars a pack."

Chapter Nineteen

Nina felt like she could fly home.

Not fly like the dragons on her trading cards.

Float.

Nina felt like the dragonfly that landed on a flower near the high school.

Its black body and bright blue wings were pretty against the stone path.

A dragonfly didn't worry about much, just where it would land next. People didn't scream when they saw a dragonfly or swat it away.

It must have been a happy life.

And today, Nina felt like she was a dragonfly.

This morning, she had a stack of trading cards in her backpack.

Now the stack was gone.

She only had one trading card left. It was a special one.

This didn't worry her. She would make more.

She was the trading card queen.

At home, she opened the door to find her mother in the kitchen.

Nina didn't know what to think. Her mother was smiling and washing dishes.

When she saw Nina, she hugged her and asked about the sale.

Nina hugged her mother back and said the sale was good. Then she asked about Ben.

"He's waiting for you, Nina," her mother said. "He wanted to sleep in your room. I hope that's okay."

Nina ran to her room and opened the door. Ben was sleeping. He was tiny, like a little baby bear sleeping in her bed.

Nina pulled the last trading card out of her backpack. It was for Ben, from Josh. It was the card of Nina with a cape and crown. She placed on the bed next to Ben and kissed his cheek. She smelled the peanut butter and saltines on his breath.

Nina lay down next to her brother. She didn't want to be anywhere else in the world. She listened to her mother and grandmother talk in the kitchen. They fried onions and peppers for dinner.

"My Nina," Ben said. He was still sleepy.

Nina kissed his cheek.

"Welcome home, Ben," she said.

Welcome home. It really felt like home.

Nina smiled.

Everything was going to be okay. Everything was really going to be okay.

About the Author

Sandra Morris is a contributing author to the Storyshares library.

About the Publisher

Storyshares is a publisher focused on supporting the millions of teens and adults who struggle with reading by creating a new shelf in the library specifically for them. The ever-growing collection features content that is compelling and culturally relevant for teens and adults, yet still readable at a range of lower reading levels.

Storyshares generates content by engaging deeply with writers, bringing together a community to create this new kind of book. With more intriguing and approachable stories to choose from, the teens and adults who have fallen behind are improving their skills and beginning to discover the joy of reading. For more information, visit storyshares.org.

Easy to read. Hard to put down.